This book is dedicated to my daughter Nowele, who is my heartbeat, my son Nadir, who is my breath, my husband, Abdelhak, who is my everything, and my father, Brad, who put the twinkle in my eye!

"There are only two lasting bequests we can hope to give our children. One of these is roots, the other, wings."
– unknown

written by Cherie Rechka
illustrations by David Mills

I heard a strange noise and what did I see?
Something was poking a hole in my tree!

I looked out my window that sunny spring day,
And saw a small woodpecker pecking away.

I named him Willie and his head is red.
His mate is Winnie and just like I said,

He worked all day to build his nest.
He hardly had any time to rest.

Back and forth he worked so hard
Each day returning to our yard.

At last he was finished and flew to his mate
But when he returned, it was too late!!

He built a nest with all his might
Then mean birds stole it which isn't right.

Some Starlings had come and stolen his nest
And I was so angry I just couldn't rest.

The Starlings were making their own nest in there
And all we could do was just stop and stare.

I couldn't sleep because I was mad
Those Starlings made me very sad.

I thought and thought about what was right.
I kept on thinking all through the night.

It isn't right to act all tough
And steal someone else's stuff.

When the Starling flew out I knew my role
Was to punish those mean birds and plug up the hole.

I felt so bad I wanted to cry.
Willie, please come back and give it a try.

Several days passed with no birds in sight.
I checked the window from day until night.

Then Willie was back without a sound
And before too long a new hole was round.

Willie came in the morning, he worked all day
And when he was finished, he again flew away.

Can you believe that around day four
Those Starlings came back and stole it once more!!

Again, we took mud and filled up the hole
So the Starlings could not keep what they stole.

We waited for days and then we were glad
Because we saw Willie and he wasn't mad.

Yes, Willie came back, to save the day.
We hope this time he's here to stay.

He started to work and Winnie came too
To help with the nest, NOW they knew what to do.

Each day he worked and had no rest.
This nest was going to be the best.

He would bob his head then in he'd go.
When he came back out, it was nice and slow.

They worked on their nest for another week
But they'd fly away if I tried to peek.

Willie, she said, stop fooling around!
Do you expect me to lay my eggs on the ground?

He would work on the nest and call her twice
Then off he flew, it was really quite nice.

They took turns guarding and fixing their place
And before too long they had enough space.

Willie perched on a branch and he looked so proud.
He chirped something to Winnie nice and loud.

She looked at her mate and she said to Willie
"I love this nest, stop being so silly".

Now Winnie stays in the nest most of the day
But when Willie comes back, she flies away.

She will peek out her head to say hello.
Is she aware of all the danger below?

Suddenly, a Starling came and we felt such doom
So we chased him off with a great big broom.

Then a cat came creeping near the nest one night.
It was time for bed but something didn't feel right.

There was no time for us to think or stare
So my husband ran out in his underwear!

He chased the cat because the birds come first.
If it found the nest that would be the worst!

Willie worked so hard and at last he was done.
We're happy to say, the woodpeckers won!

Things were calm and they had their routine
As we watched them daily from behind the screen.

What do you think they do in their nest?
Do they play games, or do they just rest?

Will they ever be safe? I really don't know.
Will a Starling come back, or maybe a crow?

Then a Starling appeared out of the blue
And fought the woodpeckers. I'm afraid it's true!

It was a terrible fight but they fought as a team
Chasing that Starling just like a bad dream.

I wish I could say that the woodpeckers won
But sometimes life isn't fair and not always fun.

They fought really hard but I'm sorry to say
The nest is now empty and they all flew away.

All three times they were forced to flee
So we were sure they would find another tree.

I love these birds, I really do.
Will they dare come back again, would you?

During the day I just sit and stare
Close to the window, but there's nothing there.

Sometimes I think I can hear their call
But when I check outside, it's nothing at all.

What happened next I saw with my very own eyes.
It's the absolute truth; I wouldn't tell lies!

Yes, five days later I almost cried
Because I spotted Willie right outside.

Willie came back but his nest was no more.
We had plugged the hole just like before.

Only it wasn't with mud, we just covered the "door"
So the nest was ready for him to explore.

He didn't stay long and when he flew away
We removed the plastic and he returned that same day.

He's been here with Winnie improving their home.
There's no more need for them to roam!

They still take turns staying in the nest.
Winnie sleeps there at night which is for the best.

Then suddenly Willie arrives with such flair.
It's really great the way they share.

Did you know that the dad helps too?
He sits on the eggs; it's the right thing to do.

I can't wait to see how many eggs there will be
And watch them hatch right there in my tree.

The babies will grow and learn to fly
And then we will have to say goodbye.

We will miss them so much when they fly from here
And hope they will come again next year.

Facts about Starlings and Woodpeckers

Starlings:

All Starlings come from a group of 100 birds that were released in Central Park in the early 1890's. There was a group of people who wanted America to have every bird mentioned in the works of Shakespeare (the European starling is mentioned in only one line of Henry IV, Part 1, Act 1, Scene 3 "I'll have a starling shall be taught to speak Nothing but 'Mortimer,' and give it him  To keep his anger still in motion."). Unfortunately these birds compete with our native birds and are considered to be an invasive species. That means they steal the nests of our native nesting birds. They are the natural enemy of woodpeckers. Starlings are very smart and wait until the Woodpeckers finish the nest and then chase the Woodpeckers out. They also trick the Woodpeckers by making the Woodpeckers chase them and then they quickly turn back and fly into their nest. Sometimes two or three Starlings will fight together. These birds are very aggressive and will fight until the end in a nest they want to take over. The Starlings have the advantage of having long legs and can stand over the Woodpeckers and hurt them. Once a Starling is inside the nest, it is very difficult for the Woodpeckers to get them out and they just give up. Starlings usually travel in groups and they can imitate sounds of lots of other birds.

Red-bellied Woodpeckers

Red-bellied male – the real Willie

Red-bellied female – the real Winnie

The male Red-bellied woodpecker's head is all red and the female is only half red. They have short legs. Woodpeckers have very sharp beaks and could easily hurt the Starlings, but it is not in their nature. That is why the more aggressive Starlings will win the nest every time. The Starlings are thriving because they are able to take over the nests of the Woodpeckers (after they have done all the work) and the Woodpeckers have no place to lay their eggs. Some Woodpeckers are now laying their eggs later in the year, after the Starling babies have hatched and they are not quite as aggressive.

- "Thanks to Shakespeare, the Starling Has Become a North American Nuisance" – Mike Stark, Associated Press, Monday, September 7, 2009
- The CornellLab of Ornithology, All About Birds

Acknowledgements

I would like to thank so many people for helping me get this book to fruition. First of all, I want to thank my husband, son, daughter, and my father for all of their understanding and for listening to me talk about these woodpeckers nonstop, and I mean nonstop!

Thanks to Jenny, for believing in me, encouraging me and letting me read to her kindergarten classes for the last 15 years. Thanks to my dear friend Margaret, who teared up when she read it. Thanks to my amazing cousin Amy, who is so wonderful, and has invited me to have my book in her awesome museum, Art in Bloom Gallery, in Wilmington, North Carolina. Thanks to my BFF April for our special Tuesdays and for all she does for me, to Paula for all she does for everyone, special thanks to Nathalie, Sabrina, Rebecca, Lori, Soraya, Robin, Hazel, Patti, Marcy, Anne, Maria, Béatrice, the wonderful Mrs. Weisberg, for teaching me about generosity and kindness, Luca & Graziella in Monza, Sara & her parents in Siena, Bibi, Andi & Jana, Randi, Marie-Claire and Arlette who have been such great friends to me for so many years. I also want to thank my spin teacher Laurie, and my spin buddy Anneli for making me look forward to exercising. Thank you to my Jusuru family for changing my life – you are all awesome! Thank you to my stepmother, Ilene, for all she did for us, to my brother Barry and his lovely wife Ayse, and their two boys, Jon and Jordan, to my sister, Stacey, her husband Mark, my niece Holly, and nephew Eric. Thank you to all of our family in Morocco who I miss so much. Special thanks to my son for his help with the cover and my daughter for her input. I would also like to thank all of the amazing people I have known in my life, (from Florida to Madagascar) who always give me such encouragement and make the world such a happy and interesting place for me.

Thank you, David, for bringing these birds to life with your beautiful and amazing illustrations.

Thank you Jimmy Fallon, for making us smile every weeknight. It is your absolute love and enthusiasm for your children and your family that inspired me to immortalize this story. The moment I saw the female I knew she would be named Winnie!

Thank you Drew Barrymore, for writing your wonderful book and sharing your stories. When I read that you jumped off a cruise ship, I had NO excuse not to try and self-publish this book! Sometimes you just have to go for it, right?

I also need to thank the wonderful people at Createspace for making it possible to self-publish and allowing people to make their dreams come true and for putting up with my incessant phone calls and pleas for help. They were all wonderful and I couldn't have done it without them!

Most importantly, I want to thank these remarkable woodpeckers. I never imagined I would feel such a connection to these little birds and their plight. They changed my life in so many ways. I feel privileged and honored that they shared their story with me and every morning I still go in the kitchen and look at the empty hole in the tree and it makes me a little sad. I think I will always be listening for their call.

About the Author

 I live in South Florida with my husband and little Chihuahua, named Chico. I worked for a wine importing company until I had my daughter and chose to become a stay-at-home mother. Books have always been important to me and I read with my children every night until they started middle school. We love to travel and have taken our children on numerous trips, including a road trip cross country, a rail trip through Europe, and snorkeling on Grand Turk in the coral reef. When my children left for college, I was forced to focus on other things. As an "empty nester", I guess my heart was longing for something to nurture again, so when these birds came into my life I felt a sense of responsibility, and became very aware of their daily routine. As this story unfolded in front of my eyes, I knew I wanted to share it with the world. I hope these little birds will inspire lots of children to pursue their dreams and never give up! Publishing this little book was truly a labor of love. Please feel free to share your thoughts and comments. You can contact me at winnieandwille@gmail.com or visit their facebook page, winnieandwillie.

Please feel free to draw your own woodpeckers on this blank space